How to Talk to Crazy People = Do Not Know

By Donna Kay Cindy Kakonge

@ Donna Kay Cindy Kakonge

How to Talk to Crazy People = Do Not Know

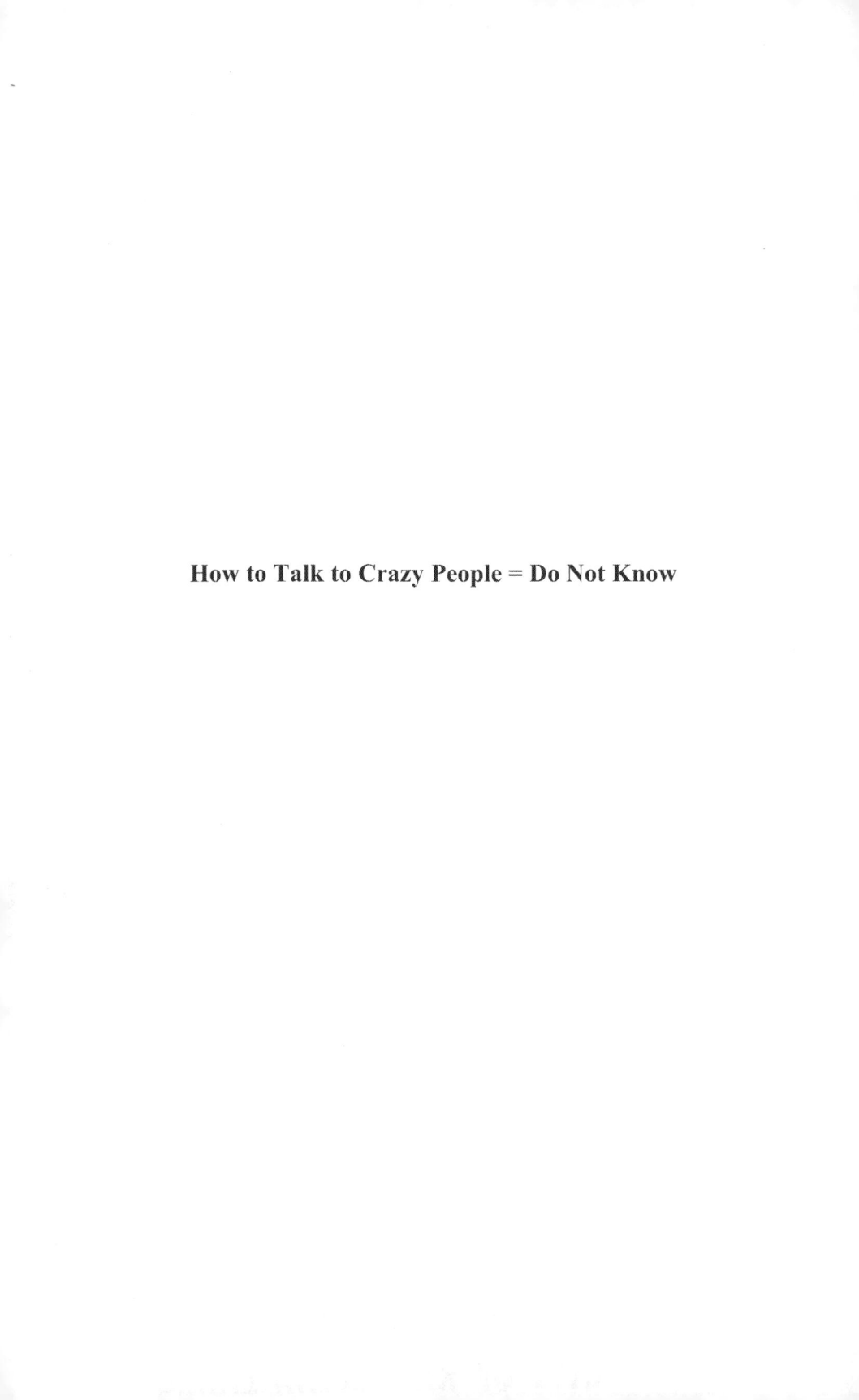

Cataloguing for Publication

ISBN: 9781072206972

Published in Canada

Dedication

To all of those people who have had even one bad day in their lives.

Angels on the ceiling and blood on the walls

I knew I was in trouble when they would not let me leave. I was locked inside a small room inside a hospital and the doctors would not let me out. I screamed, I yelled, I prayed, but it was no use – they still would not let me out.

Everything about the place was strange to me. I had not been in a hospital since I was five years old. I wanted to be home. I wanted to be back in my little apartment, drinking wine and listening to Sade tapes. I was a peaceful person. I meditated every day, I jogged six times a week, and what was I doing here?

I stayed in that room for what felt like days; I don't know how long it was. The security guard outside the door kept looking at me so strangely. "What was he looking at? He was the strange one." Couldn't he understand that this was a national emergency? I had to get out of this room because the women were coming to get me. Oprah and Princess Toro were a group of powerful and strong women who were about to rule the world and save it from disaster. Had not any of them ever read W.E.B. Du Bois? They needed to release me from this holding cell so I could reign once more back in Uganda where I was a princess and part of this 'gifted 10.' I had to go back to the country to rule, to be part of the world's ruling elite.

Then the doctors came. I knew they were doctors because they were wearing white lab coats.

"Do you know how long you've been in this state?" one of them asked as they both came in the room.

"I'm not in any state I just need to get out of here," I said.

"We can't release you until you calm down."

"Calm down, I'm perfectly calm."

Actually I was not calm, I was raging. My insides were churning and my thoughts were racing I was convinced that I needed to think quickly in order to get myself out of there.

"Do you realize that you've been screaming for an hour?" the woman doctor asked.

There was a man and a woman doctor both of them was white like ivory – ready to pierce me. Did they not realize I was screaming because they were detaining me?

I did not want to be here. I had committed no crime. I had committed mistakes, but no crime. The biggest mistake I had ever made was getting too close to my nosy landlord; he was the one who put me in this hospital, along with my father. It was both of their faults why I was in here.

I didn't even know what day it was; it was probably Halloween, 1995. What I did remember was the last time I talked to Constance; she was my psychic and tarot counselor. She had told me that my contract at a public television station was going to be renewed for months now and I had believed her. Constance was always right which took me a long time to accept, but it was true. I had met Constance almost a year ago in Ottawa, after I graduated from Carleton University.

I was a big skeptic at first but my best friend referred her to me. Constance was not just a psychic; she was a tarot counselor which really made a difference.

Constance dealt out the cards for me and she did not just tell me my future, she gave me advice and tried to help to steer me in the right direction. At the time I went to her I needed some steering.

It was a few months after I graduated from university and I had landed a great job at a public radio station – CBC. The worst thing about my great job was that it was in Toronto and my boyfriend of three years was in Ottawa. After two months of working there the great job became not so great. The hours were horrible. I would have to wake up at 3 a.m. to go to work, then I would be home by noon, then I would have to get ready to go to work for 8:00 p.m.

Have you ever tried sleeping in the daytime? It's almost impossible when you're living in a cockroach-infested basement apartment with a family of five living overhead. I was not sleeping, always scratching and forever aching for my boyfriend.

So I quit the not-so-great job and moved back to Ottawa only this time I was a worker instead of a student. Things were supposed to have been happily ever after but they got worse.

My new job at a video co-op was just as bad if not worse than the radio job. The hours were better but they were long. I had no time to see my boyfriend and when I did get a bit of time he was too busy to be with me. This was supposed to be the man I was going to marry and our relationship was falling apart.

On top of everything I was spending too much time and getting too emotionally involved with a married man who was a co-worker.

I needed guidance so I turned to Constance. All my other friends had left Ottawa after school and I needed fast answers that I could not get from a therapist.

I imagined that Constance would look like a gypsy, have her place all-dark with lots of candles and have beads hanging from the doorway. She was costing me $130 so I expected the works. She turned out to be a petite, South Asian with long black hair and jet black eyes.

Her home was filled with light and she only had one candle burning. She was not a gypsy at all. She turned out to be a lawyer who only did the tarot cards in her spare time. She did not advertise like some psychics do. She believed that those she is meant to help are guided to her.

I shuffled the tarot cards while thinking of my question. Then cut the deck. She folded out the pretty pictures and read them. She used her psychic powers to decipher what the cards meant in my life. She told me a lot of things I did know, and something I did not know. She told me I would be getting a job offer from a woman and that a man was going to lead this woman to me.

This indeed happened a week later. She also advised me not to tell my boyfriend about the married man I was spending so much time with. She told me to imagine light around me and gave the name of two books to read, Louise Hay's *You Can Heal Your Life* and *Spiritual Growth* by SANAYA Roman. It turned out that I had a book called *Personal Power through Awareness* by SANAYA Roman that I had bought and never read. A black therapist I had gone to while I was in second-year University had recommended it.

Constance also told me to meditate and while meditating to ask my high-level guides for things. Constance believed that everyone had guides and that channeling our guides could help us in our life.

She called herself a channel and that she was channeling high-beings that were helping me. She said that everything she did was channeled.

The job offer turned out to be in Toronto so I spent a lot of money on long distance calls with Constance over the next year. I also broke up with my boyfriend Alistair – or he broke up with me when he found out about the married man by reading my journal.

I began to ask Constance questions about every part of my life, such as what should I wear? Where should I live? and about my co-workers. I could give Constance a name and she could tell me about that person from the name.

This information really helped me to decide whom I was and was not going to spend time with. She told me that I could learn to be a channel and a psychic so I could answer my own questions. I bought several books after those first two.

I began meditating every day and became a vegetarian like Constance was. I wanted to be just like Constance, she was the happiest person I knew.

The doctors were getting on my nerves. They kept asking me such silly questions. I looked up to notice my father pacing outside of the small room. They were not listening to me; they seemed intent on not listening to me.

"How long are you going to keep me locked up here?" I screamed at them.

"Until you calm down," he said.

They would not even tell me why I was being locked up. After I had spoken to Constance last Friday I went on a shopping spree. She told me to make a list of all my wants, then to cut them up so that they would be on small pieces of paper. Then she told me to go into a meditation and then burn all the pieces of paper. She said this would bring everything I wanted to me. It sounded like a witch's trick and I knew that Constance was into witchcraft. So I was going to give it a try but I needed supplies first. I bought a gold pen, scissors, paper, a cup to burn the pieces in and a table. After that I had one hundred dollars left in my bank account with rent due and no paycheck coming. I went home with all my stuff and started by writing down all my wants.

I want a successful career as a diversity producer.

I want a beautiful man to enter my life and for us to have a deep and passionate relationship together.

I want a big, spacious and beautiful apartment with low rent as soon as possible, with lots of privacy.

I cut up all these wants into small pieces. I went into a meditation, asking for my high-level guides to assist me and then I burned the pieces of paper. I continued my meditation for what became days. I also decided to heighten the spiritual experience by not eating and fasting. I only drank water. I thought about a lot of things while I was meditating, and a lot of things happened to me.

The doctors forced me out of the small room and into a hospital bed on the psychiatric floor. My father came to visit me, smelling high of cologne. He told me that I must only look at the last two years to explain my breakdown (at least that is what I was calling it). He told me that he had a nervous breakdown too at sixteen while he was at boarding school. He told me that his late brother John had a breakdown too.

So the doctors kept their promise, I stayed in the hospital until I calmed down, it took a week. My mother and sister came to get me, they did not understand what had happened to me, and I did not understand it either. I went to live with my mother after that and during October 1995, Halloween of this first breakdown, to February of 1996; I was in the hospital five times. I no longer speak to Constance.

It's now twelve years later from that first break with reality. I've lost count how many other times it has happened. That expression "take a pill" applies to me.

Airport Flirt

It took an old man to touch my young breast to wake me up. I did not hear him come up to me as I sat in a plastic waiting chair because my Walkman blasted "Keep on Moving" from my Soul II Soul CD. I was in concourse E of Miami's airport, waiting for my flight to Barbados. I was coming from Montreal in the February winter wonderland and did not know how to dress. I wore a beige cotton knit ensemble with my black winter jacket curled over my arm. I was also wearing the burgundy slightly padded bra I got for Christmas from my sister. The old man had touched more foam than flesh.

"How dare you!" I shouted to his wrinkled sandy face. "Screw off or I'll call security."

He smelled of stale cigarette smoke and similar to a scent that oozed from my kitchen sink in my apartment in Notre-Dame-de-Grace, Montreal. He did not say a word as he hid the offending hand and turned to walk away. I watched him walk over to a pretty woman with white hair and a generous nose. Why he would touch me when he had her, I thought.

I found myself asleep again in the plastic chair, listening to my CD until my stomach started to growl.

I like healthy foods, but they are hard to find when you are on the go – like when you are in an airport. I had to settle on Burger King. But the Burger King in concourse E was the nicest one I had ever been in. It had this space age design and looked like a restaurant you would see on Star Trek, with rounded windows surrounded by light and aluminium. Plus, it had platinum-looking tables and chairs. I ordered a fish sandwich and some orange pop, the contents I could already see rotting inside of me, instead of nourishing me like food is supposed to do. The thing about junk food is that it is addictive. After I finished the BK food I started to crave chocolate. I had some Laura Secord white chocolate in my bag that was a gift for my Aunt Claire who was one of the people I was going to Barbados to see. The other was my Uncle Frank. I regretfully had nothing for my Uncle Frank who told me the only thing he wanted was for me to be there. Usually, when people say that I think they are lying, but not this time. He was my favourite uncle, but I had not seen him in twenty-one years. The last time I saw Uncle Frank, who was really my great-uncle on my mother's side, it was when my mother and I went down to St. Vincent for my grandmother's funeral. My mother did not want to stay in my grandmother's house because it was too painful for her, so we stayed at my Uncle Phil (who has now passed on to the other world). Not only did my mother and I have to deal with the death of a loved one like my grandmother, but we also had to deal with my cousin Carry, Uncle Phil's son, stealing our Canadian money from us. We had come down in such a hurry that there was not enough time to get traveller's cheques and Carry wanted the money to get out of St. Vincent to come to Canada. He hated the island, but his father told him he could only leave if he paid his own way. Well, he found a way.

I had a great time with Uncle Frank, and it is this experience that made this man my favourite uncle. It was also the first time I had met him and we hit it off wonderfully. "You have the gift of gab, darling," Uncle Frank told me. "Thank you, I did not know that," I told him. I was five years old. We went golfing, he took us to the beach and he splashed water in my face. He took us to great restaurants. And he always paid for everything, he always insisted on this. He would give a lot of wonderful things that were absolutely free, like kisses and hugs. He was a tall, strapping, good-looking man, who could charm a rock and probably had. I looked up to him. And although when my mother and I left Barbados and returned to Canada I never really kept in touch, he never left from having a special place in my heart. Now I was going to see him again after all these years. Many things have changed for me since five years old, and I wondered what if anything had changed for him. I knew a few things; such as he had retired after a life as a doctor, an electrician in his youth, and a soldier in the Canadian army. He was selling his house, which I remembered as being beautiful, to spend more time in his condominium in Toronto and with his daughter in the Bahamas. Now I was going to spend a week with him and his wife of fifty years in a place where twenty-one years ago I had the time of my life at a time that was also one of the saddest. I felt lucky to be getting this free break from graduate school Uncle Frank was paying for the trip. The last time I had been on a real beach was in Bahamas with my ex-boyfriend.

One night on that beach with him, just sitting in lounge chairs letting the water lap to our feet, it had been one of the most spiritual moments of my life. I really looked forward to being on the beaches of Barbados, and just being in summer again, that was truly when I thrived.

"Last call for flight seventeen-hundred," I heard from the loud speaker.

I had not even heard the first call, and I did not have my Walkman on anymore. I grabbed my stuff and ran to the gate.

Alan

I was living off of OSAP money, and needed to get a job, so I went to Toronto, visited my parents, looked for a job with newspapers and met Alan.

Alan is this six feet six inches Haitian man who I met at a library in the Annex. He came up to me, and I felt a trust for him right away, giving him all the phone numbers I could so he could reach me. That was on a Thursday, I heard from him by Saturday.

He was from Montreal, living in Toronto going to school and wanting to become a record producer. We took a walk around ASHBRIDGE'S Bay by the Beaches, and he drove me to the train station on my way back to Montreal. Then we spent a few weeks on e-mail, with him professing his love for me and telling me he wanted to marry me. He was working freelance with a company that did jingles for commercials, so he took a month off work to visit me in Montreal.

Things were going well for a few days until we went to a park near my house and made some confessions. He told me he was married. A marriage of convenience so he could get a Trinidadian girl her permanent resident status in Canada. He was paid twenty-five thousand dollars. Considering the money and my student debt load, I almost understood his decision. I told him I suffered from depression and I was taking medication. And that is when the trouble started.

We began fighting every week for the month he was there. He could not get over the fact I was taking medication and kept calling me crazy. He kept encouraging me to get off the medication, which by this point I had discovered that it was helping me. I was stressed out about finding a job for the summer, and he discouraged me on that, doubted all my plans, but did encourage me to start my own radio station on the Internet. He made a song for me, and we made up. He called me crazy again, was a lousy lover and we broke up.

I was not going to put up with any man who got off on me, and did not reciprocate. When we would argue, he would talk constantly tell me about everything I was doing wrong. About how he hated all these "black bitches" in Canada and he was just going to go to Haiti and find him a woman there. He was of typical marrying age I guess, about thirty-two. He acted like a two year-old when angry.

He was giving me a huge headache, so I kicked him out of my house in the pouring rain. As he left, I opened my drapes to make sure he was gone. Later he said he knew I really cared about him because I looked out the window when he left. Hah!

Days later, I started having regrets about the way things ended, and I had already told all my friends that he was "the one" for me. Maybe in a way to save face, I phoned him and tried to reconcile. He turned me down. I was not hurt, and did not care, and was actually relieved. I just did not want to be the one ending things. I gave him the decision, and that was like my present to him.

But later on, he changed his mind. And he kept calling me months afterward, which I still had call display, so I never answered the phone.

Right after I broke up with Alan, I had another breakdown, because I did go off my medication. This time I was put in the Brief Therapy Unit and only stayed three days because I got a job with a CBC television show for youth. That job did not last long because I had a panic attack while on the job and the best advice my boss gave me was to go back to Montreal and find some little job. So, I took his advice, in a way. I did go back to Montreal and maintained some equilibrium with mania, enough to finish my research paper for my master's degree. I was so high I wrote ninety pages in a night and finished. I also found a little job as an Announcer/Producer on an African morning show airing from Montreal.

Strategic Intentions

Eighty thousand dollars is a lot for a thirty year-old to lose. It was madness. It was the summer of 2003 and I had just ended up in the hospital again. I have bipolar disorder.

I had broken up with my fiancé and I started exercising a little too much and I think it wore down on my system. So, I ended up in the hospital and whom did I meet? I meet a guy named Frank.

He was round and bald with gray hair – very different from me. As he came down the hall he was wearing all white. He looked like he was wearing all white, a big cherub. Umm, very pale skin. Quite different from me – I have dark skin, not too fat, more voluptuous and I am tall.

We looked absolutely like opposites. What I later found out is that we were opposites, but similar in some respects.

He gave me a flower from the front counter of the psych ward. I rejected it at first, but flowers are very important to me. I love them, so I thanked him. I was in the acute ward, he was in the willing-to-roam-free ward and, um, through this glass window we ended up - we ended up - seducing one another so to speak. We played a game of show me yours and I will show you mine.

First…it started I showed him my leg. He showed me his leg. Then, I showed him my shoulder, he showed me his shoulder. I showed him my breasts, he showed me his pecks. He was such a fat man that his pecks almost looked as big as my breasts. Then, hum, I showed him the hair on my vagina, he showed me his penis. The courtship was on.

So, once I got out of the acute ward it ended up that I was in the same room Frank had been in, but he had left the hospital. He had fought with the help of a lawyer to get out. He came to visit me and kept saying I needed to get out of the hospital.

At this time I was getting visitors from friends and family. Even my former fiancé came.

I did not want to go back home, but on the day I was discharged there was a robbery at my Dad's house. They had a gun. My Dad was hit over the head with the gun and I was terrified of going home. So, I called Frank and Frank said I could come by his place. I took a cab there and Frank paid for the cab and hum, I could not believe the mess this man lived in. Small little apartment in Yorkville and we ended up sleeping together.

Me, thirty, Frank, seventy-two – him Jewish, me, Christian – him, white, me, black…Frank wanted me to convert, said we were married just because we slept together. He would sleep with the radio on, either the jazz station or the classical station. I do not think he was taking his medication. I was taking mine openly.

Frank had a complication of health problems. He had heart disease, coupled with diabetes and bipolar disorder. He had gotten into the hospital because he was trying to start a business and it was driving him mad. When he was walking around in the chill and snow of winter in his bare feet, the ambulance picked him up.

I first entered the hospital February 20, 1995. It was very cold in Toronto. Frank brought me some warmth. We had a bit of a love den. And the first time we were together we would spend all our waking hours together and all our sleeping hours together.

We went around Yorkville and he would tell me about how he had all these different businesses and money offshore. I must say the greedy part of me was kind of happy to be with a man who had money. Even though Frank lived in a small bachelor apartment in Yorkville, he told me how he had worked in a bank for thirty-five years and he had gone to law school at the University of Toronto, but he did not finish. And hum, I do like educated and accomplished men. I like beautiful men too. How could a seventy-two-year-old man be beautiful?

Frank was not. He had big watery eyes, hazel I think…definitely hazel. He had these juicy red lips…definitely juicy. He had this habit of eating every two hours because he said he needed to eat a lot. He would drink a lot. Not alcohol. I had only seen him drink alcohol once. He would drink a lot of Coca-Cola. We spent a lot of time together and then he started talking about marriage. He said he wanted to marry me. He would tell me all these different stories about his days of trying to get work in Toronto and being Jewish, it was hard. So, he went down to the Bahamas and worked for Scotiabank.

He had been married twice. His first wife he had two kids with, men older than me - and his second wife died walking off a curb and falling on her head.

He showed me places where he did work in Toronto, in the rat race of Bay Street. He showed me Kensington Market, told me that it used to be a Jewish NEIGHBOURHOOD and the one he grew up in. He was a tender man and a man who was very generous. He brought me into his home and took care of me. He made our meals. Hum, never expected me to lift a finger. He had somebody come in to clean the place. Somebody came in to take care of his feet because they were still bruised. The reason why I only lasted at the job I eventually got for a week is because Frank presented me with some papers where he said he would pay me seventy-eight thousand dollars a year to be his administrative assistant. Meanwhile, I am thinking this man has money so I thought that was the better deal…more money, good for me. He had this idea that we would do the business and I would invest the start-up costs because his money was tied up offshore. However, I would get all the money back plus my salary. So hum, I quit the job and ended up working for Frank. Working for Frank meant everything from tying his shoelaces after he would pee in his pants hidden by a bus shelter, cleaning his bum and drawing baths for him, hum, and hum, typing up documents for him. I am moving up in the job activities the job description here. And hum, having wonderful dinners with PR consultants and modeling agents at the Sutton Place Hotel to discuss Frank's idea to start an airline in Canada that would run from Toronto Island Airport. This was before the one that is there now. Passengers would only be allowed one piece of luggage and no food would be served, but food would be allowed on the plane. The bonus is that the passengers would receive really cheap discount flights.

It was called Air Sky. Frank even had one of the people hired as one of the managers of the airline make a toy plane with the Air Sky logo on it to be given to children on the plane. When I was having a party in one of the suites of The Sutton (they had cheaper rates because of SARS), my old friend Liza and her fiancé was there and when Liza saw the toy plane, she asked Frank - is that your first plane for your airline? Frank said nothing. Liza told me I did not need Frank. I did not need his debt.

As part of the spending spree for business necessities that I bought with the backing of Frank's cheques drawn on U.S. banks, so the bank was holding them for twenty-one days – bought plenty of clothes at Holt Renfrew and The Bay on Bloor to maintain the image Frank wanted me to project.

I bought a 1997 British Racing Green Jaguar with a cream leather interior and a six CD changer. It was a Vander plus. I put a ten thousand dollars deposit on a condo in Rosedale that Frank told me he would give me in writing the agreement to buy back from me with more money in my pocket.

To relax after all that shopping, I paid for a massage at some swanky spa in Yorkville for both of us, known as the Pacific Wellness Institute.

Frank left Toronto to do some business in Florida and promised he would be back in four days. He said in the meantime I could stay in his old studio and by time he came back all cheques he gave me would clear and he would have the money he needed to help me pay off the rest of the down payment on the condo.

Four days turned into four weeks until I heard anything from Frank again. He called me from jail in Jacksonville, Florida and reeled off a list of instructions that I barely listened to. I hung up the phone while he was in mid-speech. He had been arrested for fraud and I realized that is exactly what he had done to me. Every CHEQUE he gave me bounced – every single one. And I was big-time broke and without a job.

I started art modeling, worked for the government, did freelance journalism and now I teach communications and write.

Breakthrough

After my third breakdown which took place after Christmas of 1995, I spent the New Year in the hospital. Then something remarkable happened. I got a call from the *CBC National TV* newsroom calling me in for an interview to be an editorial assistant. I was still in hospital when I went into the interview with one of the bosses who ran the newsroom.

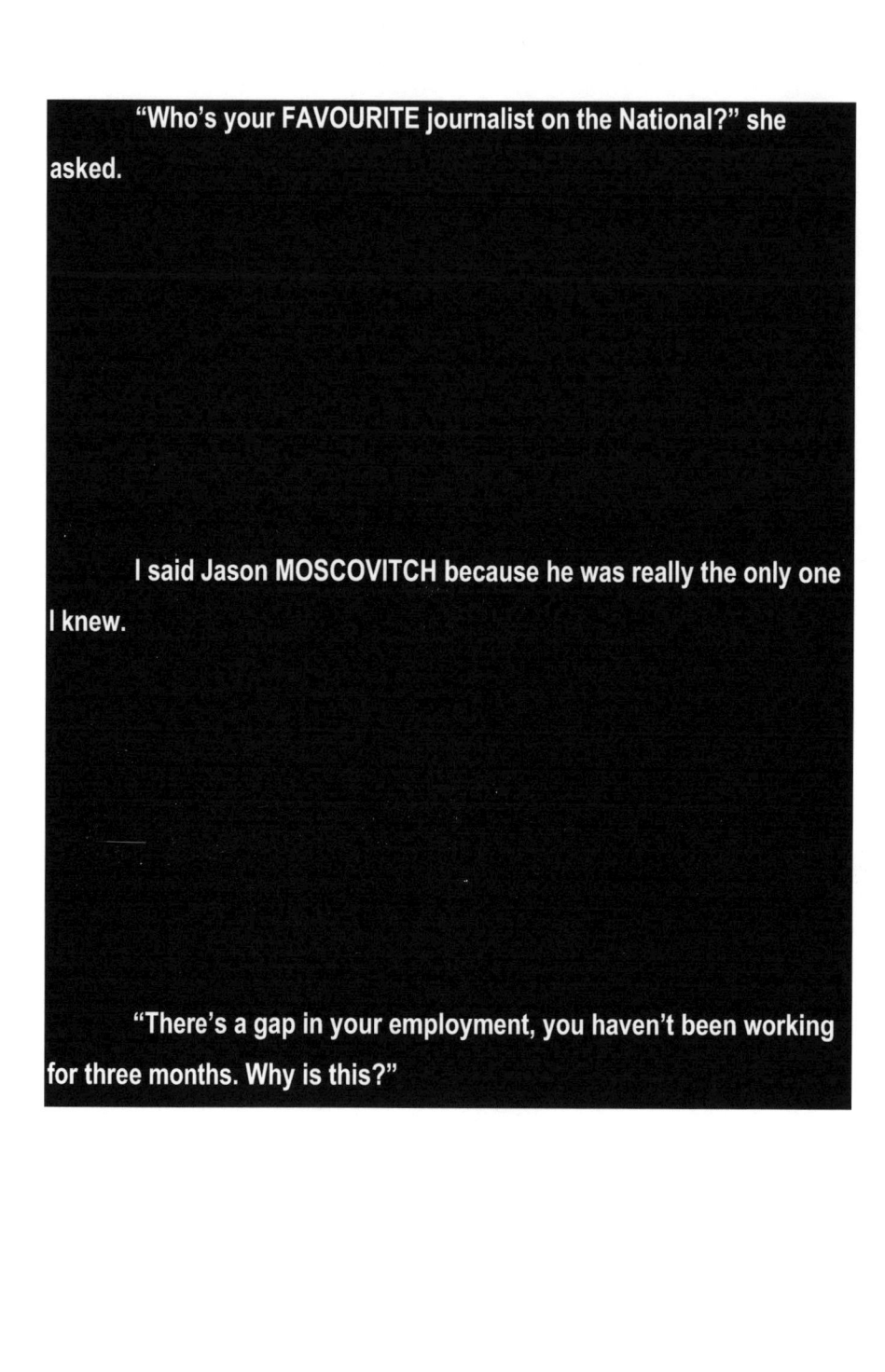

"Who's your FAVOURITE journalist on the National?" she asked.

I said Jason MOSCOVITCH because he was really the only one I knew.

"There's a gap in your employment, you haven't been working for three months. Why is this?"

Rather than tell her some elaborate lie, or just tell her I could not find work because the latter has not ever been a problem for me, I told her the truth – or at least half of it.

"I've been suffering from depression. I actually came out of the hospital just to be at this interview."

She was very understanding and said that many women suffered from this. Her assistant, Carolyn, became a friend of mine. And called me a few days later to tell me I had the job despite the stiff competition.

> **My doctor was thrilled. He was a Ghanaian man who had diagnosed me with SCHIZO-AFFECTIVE disorder, a cross between maniac depression and schizophrenia. My friends like Steven, William, and Nancy were thrilled too. I was back at the CBC and should be happy about it. The doctor said jobs gave people a purpose.**

I was greatly disappointed. The job I had at the CBC before was working both in radio and television and my title was a journalist, even though I was setting up editorial boards on diverse communities. Now I had been downgraded to an editorial assistant. Working shift work again, and running script between newsroom and studios, as well as running the tele-prompter.

Life at home was stressful. Without my independence at the age of twenty-three LIFE, living at home when I had been on my own since undergraduate education at eighteen, was very difficult, sometimes, yet joyful! The family was shattered by my health. And my brother and sister still seemed to stay away from me.

Before, as a teenager, when I was living in my mother's house I was in the basement and had it completely to myself. For some reason then I could stand the darkness, but I was sleeping a lot and undiagnosed depressed and maniac. When I moved back into her home, my brother had a room on the third floor of the house, and he unwillingly made an exchange with me to take his room so I could have more light to lift my depression. But this was only after I broke down for the fourth time.

I was sleeping on a mattress on my mother's floor to avoid the basement and it was driving me crazy. I was still refusing to take consistently the medication the doctor prescribed, because Constance had once told me it would make me weak. I was not sleeping and still working and finding it hard to deal with the shifts, although they were not as bad as the ones in the national radio newsroom. One morning I called in sick, having a crying fit on the phone with my boss for the editorial assistants, Carolyn. That night I asked my mother for the keys to her car and left the house, driving in a maniac daze to Steven and William's house.

They let me crash there. Steven kept trying to make me food, but I would not eat. William was smoking pot while I was talking furiously and fast about being a Ugandan princess and asking the others and myself why the fuck I was in Canada when I could be a queen in Uganda. William's girlfriend was part of my audience too.

After the night was over, Nancy came by and tried to console me, because I was in a crying fit. She was dating Steven, after trying to fix me up with him. On the second night of my staying at Steven and William's place, while Steven was sleeping on the couch because he gave me his bed, I tried to seduce him. I was confused. I thought we could still be together and he was treating me so well, and I was so needy for comfort and affection.

He rejected my advances. The next day, without anything being said, Nancy and William tried to take me to a hospital in Scarborough. The doctor on staff tried to give me a whole bunch of drugs that I refused to take. And I stormed out of the hospital.

What I remember next is when Nancy and Steven tried to take care of me. I told them I wanted to go to this black bookstore in downtown Toronto around Bathurst Street that is no longer under the same management. It was a husband and wife team who owned it. When I got into the store, I sat by the books for children, sat down on a child's chair, all of my five feet ten inches and about one hundred and thirty pounds, in shoes, and cried.

Nancy and Steven took me out of the bookstore. We were driving in Steven's old Mercedes Benz in blue and went to my father's house. Nancy did not come, I do not know why.

Before we got to my father's house I noticed a house up for sale. I told Steven I wanted to buy that house and raise my brother and sister because as the eldest and with all the fighting going on in the home for so long I felt I had done that any way. Steven took me to my father who wanted me to go to the hospital, but I refused. Then, he wanted to keep me inside the house. I refused that too. When they would not let me go I threatened to jump off my father's balcony, and I swear my father almost hit me, but Steven denies witnessing this.

Steven took me away, I finally got out of my father's home, and he was driving me to the hospital. I was raging. I walked down the street to the hospital downtown ranting and raging and disturbing the dead. The police at Wellesley subway station stopped me and an ambulance took me to the nearest hospital. I was ranting at the hospital, for putting me in restraints, which is like bondage and slavery to a black person. I was ranting for them keeping me in an isolation room making it difficult for my godmother to come and visit me. I was ranting at them for my illness, because I was sick.

I stayed not long in the hospital; with medication I usually make a quick recovery. I was going to be followed by a female doctor, a psychiatrist to see every week. I still had my job at the CBC, but I was very depressed. It was a struggle for me to get up in the morning and I hated taking the medication, lithium. And now I was diagnosed as a maniac depressive, after being called a schizophrenic the first time. I got sick for the fifth time in March of 1996, the events causing my doctor at the Scarborough hospital where I was sent to chastise me. He wanted to keep me in hospital for a long time to run tests on me. My boss Carolyn from the CBC came to visit me and said she could not see what was wrong with me. She also promised me she would put me on a regular shift, the night one from six o'clock to two o'clock, where I would be like an evening researcher. This fed my ego a bit. Despite doctor's orders I signed myself out of hospital, and the Ghanaian doctor said he would never treat me if I returned to that hospital again. I wonder what has happened to him now. Perhaps those tests on my health were needed more than my job. But I chose work. And I continued to see the female doctor at the downtown hospital taking lithium until she went on sabbatical without telling me. And I got off my lithium.

I managed to stay well for six months without any medication and without a psychiatrist. I made some friends in CBC National newsroom, two of whom I knew from my undergraduate journalism degree at Carleton, such as Rosie and Diane. The other was named Mary who I trained for the job as editorial assistant.

By the spring and summer, Rosie decided she wanted to spend it in Ottawa, so she rented out her one bedroom spacious condo to me for three months for three hundred a month. The condo was perfect. All decorated in dark green like nature. I needed only to come with my clothes and it was located in the Annex, just steps away from St. George subway station. I got a chance to get my independence back and my Sunday brunches with Diane and Casey, another friend I made, made life very sweet.

There were signs that not everything was OK in my head, that in retrospect I can see. I kept imagining that someone was following me. And, that this guy who I had a crush on at work was outside my door stalking me. Wishful thinking I suppose.

I was not enjoying my job at the CBC. It was mundane and dull. I needed a challenge and made my plans to go to Uganda.

Uganda was the place I had always dreamed of going to since I was 14 years old. I remember telling my dad, and he discouraged me by telling me I would get killed. This did not deter me since he did tell me this in a drunken stupor. The only way I was going to get to go to Uganda was if I lied. So I told my dad I was going with a white friend named Emily who I also worked with at the CBC. Emily did want to go to Africa, but did not have the money to go at the time. I had my father believing Emily was going with me the whole time. He gave me money to help me go and set me up with my Uncle Edward who was head of the biochemistry department at MAKERERE University so I could be a lecturer in the mass communication department. Once everything was set, I planned to leave in October of 1996, just in time for their school year to start where I would be teaching radio and television. I gave my notice to the CBC, just before a permanent editorial assistant position was opening up, which many people felt I would get. It went to Mary, who I had trained. I planned to get other work in Uganda and hopefully do some freelancing, so I contacted media places in Toronto and bought a Hi-8 video camera so I could do video work while I was there.

I flew British Airways. My whole family said goodbye to me at the airport, and my friends from the CBC had a going-away party for me. As I boarded the plane, it seemed like I was in good mental health, without medication, and without a psychiatrist, but just by following one of my dreams.

Broadway

I lost my job at Radio Canada International in a day with only two weeks' severance. This happened May 16, 2000. I fell into a depression.

> They say the neon lights are bright on Broadway…I wanted to know. All I wanted was to get to Broadway, and I wanted to get there fast.

I was in another of my maniac phases just a few days after seeing my shrink. I fell into a depression first deciding that I was a failure in Montreal, and I was going to pack it all in and move to Toronto. There, I could be with my mother and my sister, live in my mother's house, and think over my life. There were too many pressures in Montreal. Thinking about what to do about ending my lease, trying to get unemployment insurance after losing my job at the public broadcasting radio station, plus my boyfriend Michel was a tour guide and spent a lot of time away. I was missing him and doubting his love for me at the same time.

In a crying fit I phoned him and broke up with him while he was in Toronto. He did not even sound angry. I did not give him the time to make a fuss. He did seem confused and really wanted to talk to me about it. I would not let him and hung up the phone before he could say anything else. He was just using me any way I told her.

That night I did not sleep. I started packing my things for Toronto. Wondering if I could move out first thing in the morning, I called an overnight mover to see if they could move all my furniture and things by the next day, which was a Friday. Even though I was expected to be in Ottawa to see my godmother, I was making the decision to be in Toronto instead.

I called my sister and asked her if she could pick me up at the train station. I had made the decision that I would only leave with what I could carry. She wanted to pick me up at Guildwood, but I asked her to pick me up downtown instead.

My sister thought it was better to meet at Guildwood, but I insisted on downtown. Toronto downtown at night looks like Broadway. I told her I was taking the express train from five o'clock to nine o'clock.

I started packing. I decided to take my favourite three bags and leave most of my things to make up for the rent I still owed.

I went around my apartment when I thought I could get a mover putting post-it notes on the things I wanted moved. That was similar to how they handled the move at Radio Canada International where I worked.

Once I realized I could only make this move with what I could carry, I concentrated on my three favourite bags – all black. In the large one went my clothes. My designer items fitting better a slightly smaller version of myself. I put things like magazines, Oprah Winfrey's first in my knapsack plus some of my own writing. I put my expensive mini-disc and had MY ENTIRE ID in my mailman-like Gap bag.

I did get some sleep that night, a fitful one. I dreamed that my mother went bankrupt and her and my sister went to live with my rich godmother. That dream brought me happiness and a sense that there were good things to come.

Early in the morning I remember I trekked out of my apartment carrying the three black bags. I left my door open and the key by the landlord's doorstep.

Just in case I did decide to stay in Montreal, I planned to check into a bed and breakfast on CHERRIER Street in Montreal I had seen before. On my journey there I lost my big bag with designer clothes and my own original paintings at ANGRIGNON Metro. My mind was totally messed up going to SHERBROOKE Metro and I went in the opposite direction. There were whispers of not working from my lover, feelings of regret and loss.

By time I REACHED to the Château CHERRIER, all I HAD WAS MY Gap bag and KNAPSACK. I rang the BELL, THEY let me in.

"Are you looking for a single room?" the middle-aged QUEBEÇOIS man asked.

I had broken up with Michel, so I was. "Yes."

He showed me to a clean room upstairs, no carpet on the floor, furniture bland. Before I settled in, I went to settle the money with the middle-aged man.

"I'm only staying for a few days to find an apartment in the Plateau." Even though I already had a lease signed with an apartment in VILLERAY. "I'm hoping I can get a deal on the room."

I did not have a lot of money I wanted to spend. I had to keep a float in my account for bank reasons. We negotiated the room would be one hundred dollars with tax for three days. I gave him my camera – Pentax and from my mother – as collateral in case I stayed more days.

I tried to get the middle-aged man named Lionel into a conversation about doing some redecorating for him, being able to use his computer to work on my RESUMÉ, about sex (although I had no intention to do it with him. I just wanted to talk, and to work, and be useful). All I got were the keys to my room, room three HUNDED and two, and instructions to be back by 9 p.m.

I walked the Plateau, leaving my knapsack locked in the room. I decided I did not want to live there because it was so loud. I headed for the train station remembering I was to meet my sister.

I booked a train for about three o'clock one way to Toronto. That cost me more than a one hundred dollars on my VISA. In my head it was forty dollars. I had plenty of time to kill – it was still morning. I decided to do some work.

"They say the neon lights are bright on Broadway," I sang. I was sitting on Rene-Levesque outside the train station with my hand held out for change.

I got a dollar. I voyaged through good and bad NEIGHBOURHOODS by foot and bus to make it to my bank outside L`EGLISE Metro to deposit the dollar. I asked them to put it in my CHEQUING/savings account.

Then, I went to work again. Outside L`EGLISE METRO, I sang and danced and drew a small crowd. None of them would give me money. They looked like unemployed older men and we were all in the same boat.

"You should create a real show," one of them said. "Add music and costumes and play an instrument."

I did not take his advice too kindly. I packed up my act and jumped on the metro to head back to the train station, only carrying my Gap bag.

I seemed rather sane as I boarded the train. Calmly I selected to take the train car heading to Guildwood, forgetting about my plans with my sister to meet downtown. I had given her a call to tell her I was on a different train.

I had my mini-disc with me in my one bag and I spent most of the ride listening to interviews I had done while working at the public broadcaster. I came up with this idea that one way I could make money and keep myself busy was to write a book, transcribing these interviews with interesting people.

It is funny the thing about being on medication. It keeps you regular, it keeps you sane, and it keeps you in the moment of your daily reality of everyday life. Not taking it as I traveled on that train, in retrospect I realize I was not dealing with reality of my mania. My mind was in the past, and in the future, but never really in the present moment.

When I got off the train I had finished listening to a conversation behind me. Two young men were talking about getting into graduate school and getting their PhDs. Something I could relate to having my master's degree, and also having my own PhD aspirations. They were talking about the sciences though, physics and chemistry. That I cannot relate to because both of my degrees are in arts, one being in journalism. Then the conversation switched to something else I could relate to.

The young man on the left, who I turned around to see that he was blond, started talking about his father who was schizophrenic. After I listened to his story of growing up with his father, and everything he went through, the father's struggles too, I put myself to work once again – this time through journalism and not through song.

"Excuse me," I said turning around.

I told him about being a journalist and that I wanted to do a story about his life with his father. He seemed very happily surprised, and I gave him my father's phone number so he knew where to reach me.

As I unloaded from the train I chatted with the few men, as long as some other people. I sauntered off the train saying goodbye to a middle-aged woman and a "see ya," to the young man with a schizophrenic father.

"Call me," I told him as I went out to find my sister for the ride to my mother's.

I saw no one in sight and instantly jumped into a cab to take me to my mother's, only carrying my Gap bag.

The driver in the burgundy cab and I talked about lots of things because it was a long ride home. First I wanted him to drop me by the hotel where Michel was staying as part as his work as a tour guide. He mainly lives in Montreal and it was just a temporary job until he started working with the French section of Canada's public broadcaster.

Michel was not there. He had already checked out of the hotel. I left him a note with "fuck you," scribbled on it and intended to keep it until I saw him. I kept that note in my hands all the way to my mother's house.

I no longer have the keys to my mother's semi-detached home she had in Markham, so I rang the bell. She welcomed me, but I did not really want to be there.

We got into an argument. I went into her room that looked as gothic and museum-like as that Château CHERRIER place in Montréal. I told my mother how I felt, my anger at her for putting up with a man who beat her for so many years. It hurt me the past. The room was filled with ghosts that I had grown up but still should of stayed in the past. I was not taking my medication but telling my mother that I was.

Something in my mother's eyes scared me – the hurt, the pain, the anguish as she looked at me. I ran out her door into the night with my bag. As I ran down Warden Ave., I dropped my bag. The weight was too much. And I desperately wanted to rid myself of my baggage.

I ran to the BAMBURGH Circle convenience store and tried to call my father to pick me up. I could not get a hold of him so I ran from BAMBURGH Circle in the dark night to Finch Ave.

Once I was at Finch I did not know what to do with myself. I had no money or ID, I threw that away. I thought about hitching a ride to my Dad's house, which I had not ever done before, but that was too dangerous and scared me. I saw a bus coming.

I ran across the street to the bus headed to Finch station and begged the guy to let me on. He said yes and I took a seat in the back. I was distraught, so I started to sing.

"They say the neon lights are bright, on Broadway," I sang at the top of my lungs. "They say the neon lights can fill the air."

People seemed to be happy, one guy, white, even told me to "sing on sister." So I did.

As the bus was reaching the subway station a black man was coming off and he told me to shut up. I got verbally violent with him. Jumping up like a Jamaican and telling him I was going to put a gunshot to his head. He stayed away from me.

I sang on the subway too, getting through with no problem in Toronto's Transit system. At first I sat down and sang, and then I started walking through the cars and singing, trying to get change. When I did not get any I got off at Lawrence East subway station.

I was frightened there, without any idea of where to go, I called my Dad to pick me up and meet me at the corner opposite the Coffee Time at Young and Lawrence.

I tried to wait patiently; my Dad said he would be about half an hour. While I waited, I decided to take my performance to the streets.

I sang and drew a crowd of teenagers. Plus I did a little performance art for them. The show exhausted me, I got a standing ovation, but my father still had not come, and I had no money in my pockets.

I walked down some street close to a park, thinking about sleeping in the bushes for the night. I got scared and decided to hail a cab to New York, to Broadway. A cab stopped and I got in, thanked him for stopping and told him I wanted to go to New York. I had no money and he did not want to go anyway. I had a friend in New York, married with a cat, and living in Spanish Harlem with a great job. I figured she could pay my cab and I could pay her back and crash at her place.

He decided not to take me for the ride that left me on the dark streets of Toronto alone. I was scared and manic at the same time. I saw this lovely apartment building and tried to find shelter there.

The concierge let me in and I told him I wanted a job as a doorwoman. The concierge turned me down but I sat outside the building, smoking cigarettes he had given me. I planned to wait until morning when the manager came to ask for a job.

The plan did not last long. I walked back to the corner of Yonge and Lawrence, weary of every man looking at me. My hair was in an extension with a weave at the end and even in my state, I looked like a hot mama.

I looked like a hot mama so much so that I attracted this older Greek man named Cyril at the Coffee Time corner.

I was sitting there, getting day old bagels for free from the kind South Asian owner, and coffee. I was also singing at the counter. Cyril beckoned me over. I told him to wait awhile until I finished my song.

I did not get to know his name until much later, but I found out we were alumni from Concordia University, called Sir George Williams in his time. He was an engineer and fascinating to talk to. He had been in Tanzania for eight years working there and we talked a lot about Africa.

We also talked about life in general. I was feeling very confused about where to direct my anger at the injustice in the world. The injustice of having so many crazy people in my life, people driving my family crazy, racism, sexism, lack of respect from bad people for being a stellar person, collectively with others, as well as on my own, and being out of work with my education and credentials, of having a boyfriend who in my mind did not really love me. Cyril explained it this way:

"There is a balance in life. There are no winners or losers. Who wins and who loses is a game, it's just a game. The focus must be on balance."

Master's

I came into the hospital raving about the death of my brother. Never having seen the *Blair Witch Project* I imagined that a group of witches, one of them including someone I worked with, had gone to Toronto and killed him.

The medication was out of my system and my thoughts were racing faster than I was down the street. After sitting through an information session at McGill's PhD program, I checked myself into a hotel, the most expensive one in town, and rode the bus up Du PARC on a dark Montreal night.

On the bus I spoke to the sky, looking at the crack of it coming through the escape exit on the ceiling.

"God, I will avenge my brother's death. Kevin, you are in Heaven, but I will bring your murderers to Hell."

I jumped off the bus before the driver had a chance to kick me off and marched down SHERBROOKE Street. Once I returned to the hotel, I ordered their most expensive meal, but something told me not to order the most expensive wine.

My room was large and luxurious. It had a TV that swung completely around from the bedroom to the living room. I got bored of crying and went downstairs in my white hotel bathrobe and bought some cigarettes from the front desk.

"What are you doing down here dressed like that?" the man at the desk asked.

I laughed and asked for the cigarettes. Later I realised that he must have thought what was a girl like me checking into a hotel like that – must have been a call girl.

I was having fantasies of being enormously wealthy and living them out. When he pulled out a grand box filled with different kinds of cigarettes, I laughed again and remembered when my father gave me a carton of cigarettes before Christmas 1998.

"Did my father send those?" I asked in a British accent I did not have.

The man just shook his head at me, as though I was crazy.

I did not sleep that night. In the morning, I came down again in my bathrobe to the large hotel lobby and expected to be treated like a queen. The manager got fresh with me, and was hostile towards me. He ordered me out of the hotel. The police and someone from the CLSC came. That is how I got into the hospital, once again at the Royal Victoria, once again in the Brief Therapy Unit.

Since I stayed two weeks in the hospital, I made friends there. I was trying to secure employment at Radio Canada International's new African section while in the hospital. I was also trying to set a date for my project defence.

The environment inside a hospital is hostile. There was this one woman named Carolyn who did not like me. She thought I was some spoiled rich brat. Her friend was Michele, an Italian woman who later became my roommate. Michele and I became friends and when I got out of the hospital I stayed with her for a while. But it was a manic event.

Michele devised this plan that we would go into business together. She would pay me fifty thousand dollars a year and we would do music videos. She had me stay in her apartment for a week watching music videos, shopping when we were outside, spending my own money on her, and listening to music. We went to the Bonaventure Hotel and had an expensive meal, on me. I was using my credit card and spending money I did not have. Michele was luring me into thinking I was the one to marry her brother REESHARD, who I had met in the hospital and had an instant crush on. Michele said something about my medication just being sleeping pills any ways, so why take them. I listened to her and stopped taking my medication for about a day. It made me do the strangest things at the Bonaventure Hotel.

I thought REESHARD was coming, and Michele kept saying that he was. She said there was going to be a big party for her. She told me to go to Place Ville Marie and wait for REESHARD. I went and sat there for hours, even though I had to go to the washroom, I held it. When I could not stand it anymore and I had already started peeing my pants, I left the designated spot, went to the washroom, and looked for Michele. I found her back at the Bonaventure Hotel, and we went back to her place where she had a big fuss with her boyfriend and brother who knew she was not taking her medication. When I realised that she was acting that way because she was not on her meds, I started taking my medication, and called my sweet friend David to pick me up and deal with the situation. I walked away with David, wanting him to spend the night at my place, but he had to go back to his girlfriend.

Michele ended up in the hospital. I stabilized once I started taking my medication again regularly and as prescribed. I got the job at Radio Canada International part-time, turning to full-time after the technician's strike. I also got my master's degree.

A doctor I did not like was following me in the outpatient ward of the Allan Memorial at the Royal Victoria Hospital. I started self-prescribing medication. The medication he put me on made me gain more weight, made me sleep for thirteen hours at a stretch, and generally depressed. By the early part of the millennium, I started talking to David, who is also a pharmacist, about how I could get off my medication. By March, I took myself off.

Future, Future

Part One:

    I had no idea how long I had been walking when I saw the light at the top of a house on Esplanade. Ever since I had run away from my dinner with Mary, I was just walking, not feeling safe anywhere. Mary had talked about us taking a vacation to Mexico. I even remember her saying she would pay. She made a lot more money than I did working for radio as a journalist. She did erotic massage. I was sure her job was more fun too. But, I cursed Mary for not letting me stay over at her place, when my janitor was harassing me, my father looking for me. I kept thinking they were trying to kill me, and that they had already killed my cat. I kept seeing images of my cat everywhere. It was frightening me. I had been walking around late at night, scared that something would happen, and even more scared to go home.

I took a bus to the end of the line, the woman driver screaming at me to get off. I took a cab to the corner of Mont Royal and PARC – I was looking for Kim's house – a guy I knew at work who I had dated once or twice. I was sure that I could find safety there. But, I had spent the whole night trying to find it. And, I was sure that my father had put some spell on me through the Haitians in Montreal and was messing up my mind. Just as I was coming close to being in Kim's safe house and arms, my father and his evil kind were changing the streets of Montreal to look like my hometown Toronto.

Once I got to the corner of Mont Royal and PARC with the taxi driver (who was black and I was sure was working for my father), I threw pennies at him in the busy intersection instead of paying.

I walked my way up to Mary's house, at Van Horne, the walk seeming like one to a corner store in comparison to all the walking I did that Friday, March 24, 2000. I seemed to reach Mary's in minutes and I rang the bell.

No one answered. I knew she was there and I needed to go to the bathroom so I pissed on her walkway. I was also pissed with Mary.

It is further down the street, heading towards Bernard, that I saw the light at the top of the house. I felt filthy. I had been walking like the killer in the Spike Lee movie, *Summer of Sam*. My thighs were soiled with urine, and chaffed. I had been wearing the same clothes for the past two days. I needed a shower. I walked towards the house.

I could hear music and lots of voices. I had no idea what time it was, although I was wearing a watch – I was afraid to know what time it was.

I climbed the steps to the apartment at the top where I knew the party was. I rang the doorbell and a light flickered outside. I figured this was my safe house.

Music and many strange sounds filled my senses. I took a quick look around and headed to the bathroom.

I took off all my clothes and started to draw a bath in the old-fashioned big tub. I scrubbed away at my dirty skin – thankful I had found a safe place to be.

Some of the guys at the party were trying to come in to the bathroom while I was there. Someone firmly closed the door.

When I was finished bathing, I tried to turn the water off, but could not.

Standing up out of the water naked, I went to the bathroom door and asked some of the women if they could turn the water off. One woman started laughing uproariously, and I told her to shut up, thinking she must be crazy to be laughing at a time like this.

A woman came to turn off the water and I got dressed. I moved into the mix of the party.

No one seemed to be really talking to me, a few people saying hello. I knew no one there.

I went to sit down on one of the coaches. I was surprised after I checked out the apartment. There were so many people in the kitchen that I could not get through and see a thing. The bathroom was empty now that I was not in it. The hallway had a smattering of people. There was a room in the front that I could not figure out what it was used for. There was a small balcony off that room.

I asked someone where the bedroom was in the apartment, feeling very confused. The person never answered.

In the living room, the middle was empty, but with a stereo in the corner, and two couches pushed side-by-side up against the wall along the door I originally came through. The floors were hardwood.

I sat down on a couch I remember being crème, beside a couch I remember being dark, maybe navy. I sat there and looked around for only a few minutes when I heard a deep voice in my left ear.

"Are you a friend of the hostess…"

I looked over at a white young man, with dark hair, a moustache and a goatee. He was wearing a suit – tie, yellow with stripes. I had noticed him talking with a young man with lighter hair and kind of rotund. We had smiled at each other before he said his first words to me. I had been sitting there, looking around, and feeling very safe from the evil spirits of my father.

"No, I do not know anyone here," I replied, noticing his eyes were blue. I liked that. Very exotic.

We chatted for a while, me on the crème couch, him on the dark couch. After awhile it seemed silly.

"Why don't you come sit over here…" he asked when the lighter-haired guy left to refresh his drink.

I got up and went over there to sit beside the dark-haired, blue-eyed young man, wearing a suit.

One of the very first things he did when I sat down was take off his jacket and loosen his tie.

"I don't like wearing a suit," he said. "I came here from work."

He started telling me about this journalist who interviewed him about something for work. He talked about how the journalist asked stupid questions and kept trying to turn the story into what he wanted, rather than what the story really was.

I completely agreed with him, letting him know I was a journalist and basically had a low opinion of them. Then he said:

"My name is Nicholas by the way."

I rolled the name around in my head. Nicholas was acceptable.

"I'm Karen."

He looked all nervous and kept undoing his tie until it was off.

"What does that say on your shirt…"

I was wearing a T-shirt that said 'YARI, YARI,' the meaning I had forgot. I received it at a writer's conference in New York. I knew it was in an African language and I thought it meant future, future, but I wasn't sure.

"It doesn't matter,' I said.

"Well," Nicholas unbuttoned the highest button on his shirt.

"I'm just trying to make conversation and I'm interested in what it means."

He needed to repeat himself a few times because I couldn't hear him over the music and voices.

"It doesn't matter." I refused to give a possibly incorrect translation of yari yari.

"It's just that," he undid another button, "I saw you in the bathroom, and all these guys were looking at you. I didn't want them to look at you so I shut the door."

"Uh-hmm…" I moaned, wondering what else the night had in store for me.

"I'm the one who shut the door."

I nodded my head and looked at him occasionally. I had made the right choice sitting beside Nicholas. The right choice in the man who would help me keep sane.

Nicholas told me that he had been the one to close the bathroom door because he liked me, and found me attractive. I found Nicholas attractive too, and it was getting too loud at the party to carry on a good conversation. I suggested we leave.

"Do you want to go to a café where we can talk?" I asked.

He looked pleasantly surprised.

"Sure, we could go to a café."

Nicholas seemed to debate the issue of getting a coffee for five minutes before finally getting up the courage to get his jacket and wait by the door for me. Neither of us really knew anyone at the party – and we wanted to get to know each other – so making a party of two seemed to be the solution.

I enjoyed the walk with Nicholas. We both walked increasingly closer to each other, with our hands fidgeting in our pockets. It was a beautiful late March evening – more worthy of early summer in Montreal, than early spring.

I decided to change the coffee in a café to tea at his place. I popped my medication and vowed to keep taking them for the rest of my life. I was curious what his place was like, and I needed a safe place to stay.

He asked me if I wanted anything, I cannot remember what I said. But we stopped off at a depanneur in the taxi we took to his place. I waited in the taxi and Nicholas left and came back like magic. I had to keep looking at him in the cab to make sure it was him.

We had to be very quiet as we climbed the steps to his apartment on the top floor. It was beautiful, a huge three-and-a-half by Montreal standards – a huge one bedroom for Toronto. In Toronto he could easily spend one thousand dollars a month on rent. I did not ask, but I was sure he was paying about half that amount.

The walls were filled with huge paintings – kind of rustic, but showed a good eye. Nicholas brought me to the kitchen.

"Do you like the table?"

"Yes, it's beautiful."

"I made it," he said.

I looked at him with shock. "You're a carpenter, like Jesus." Now I knew why he was saviour.

"Actually, I designed it. I picked out the pattern and the style and gave that to the people who did the physical labour."

It was a beautiful table. Dark red and golden tiles almost looked like stained glass on the table top.

"You're an artist," I said.

"Here," he said, taking my hand into the living room. It was the first time we had touched, and I did not know how I felt about it.

"See these paintings on the walls, and the photographs? Who do you think did them?"

I turned to him and smiled, "you."

He nodded.

They looked even better now that I knew he was the artist.

He fell asleep, and I roamed about the apartment until morning light. I threw the black magic woman cat outside. I carefully studied every piece of art and photographic art on the walls, absolutely impressed. By time the morning light came, I was convinced this was the man I had been looking for most my twenty-seven years.

It was a Saturday, but he had to go to work for a meeting at 11. I lied in bed while he got dressed.

"I could stay here," I offered.

"No, I don't think that's a good idea. I'll call you later."

I gave him my phone numbers, at work, at home, and on my pager. I never took his number because I was angry he would not let me stay in his apartment.

By time we stepped outside the triplex, mastering the three flights of stairs, I was not angry anymore and just happy it was daylight, and I could occasionally look into his blue eyes.

I had no idea where we were, but we walked to the Metro (the subway station) which about 10 minutes.

Once we were on the train, we had a light conversation, Nicholas saying we should wait two years with our relationship and see if it can go anywhere after that. Last night he was talking about other relationships he had, and how his work always got in the way. I did tell him about having bipolar disorder, and he kept encouraging me to smile.

Nicholas got off at Peel station, and I expected to see him again soon. He asked me what I was doing for the day. I told him I would go home and try looking for another apartment.

That is not exactly what I did that day. I never ended up at home, but I did find shelter at the Royal Victoria Hospital on the psychiatric ward for about ten days.

Almost ten years later I take my medication every day – I write this as I listen to Alanis MORRISETTE singing "Ironic." This is my long song with a quiet title of "Manic.

Made in the USA
Middletown, DE
24 July 2019